"We have a super-duper, THRILLING, outing planned,' chirped Miss Wilderness, as grey drizzle trickled down the classroom window and gloomy clouds gathered to loom glumly over Libby's dull old, dreary old town.

Gloomy clouds

dull puddle

dog mess

Very ordinary houses

'Humph,' thought Libby. 'I expect it's going to be a trip to a super duper cement factory. Or somewhere they make thrilling paper clips, or one of those museums with lots of little piles of stone and old fluff and notices saying DO NOT TOUCH. '

Whenever grown-ups said anything was going to be exciting it usually meant a day visiting a great aunt with

no teeth who smelled of stale tea-bags,
or a squawking dribbling baby you
were supposed to be nice to, or a family
wedding, where you had to sit still for days
while vicars droned on. Libby was going
to such a wedding only next week. It was
her cousin Gertie's wedding and Libby was
dreading it. No one had even asked her to
be a bridesmaid.

So when Miss Wilderness went on to say,

'We are going to have a whole weekend out at Pirate Palace,' Libby was amazed. Pirate Palace was the fantastic new theme Park that had opened a few miles outside Bleak-on-the-Common and Libby had been begging her mum to take her there for weeks.

'Cool,' whistled Brainy Billy King. 'It's got the highest scariest steepest roller coaster in the world.'

'And you'll be able to recite your sixteen times table backwards in it,' said skinny

Yasmin, waggling her ears at Billy.

Wish I could do that, thought Libby. She meant the wiggling the ears bit, not the times tables bit. She was in a bad mood. A very bad mood. A disgusting mood. All day her head had felt as if it was on fire. It was itching so badly it felt like poor Miss Wilderness must have felt when Naughty Nigel sprinkled itching powder in her jumper.

'Aren't you excited about the Pirate Palace?' asked Libby's sort-of best friend Karen at break time. 'It'll be, erm, exciting, won't it?' Karen continued bravely, although Libby could see she wasn't in the least bit excited. Poor old Karen-next-door hated scary rides. Karen was alright in a normal sort of way but, with her neat little shoes and socks and her carefully ironed dresses, she was just a bit, well, boring. Like me, I suppose, thought Libby, as she longed,

Karen-next-door

not for the first time, to be best friends with sporty Barbara, who could somersault backwards, or ear-waggling Yasmin. Or even Brainy Billy King, who really could say his sixteen times table backwards while skateboarding.

'Yes, of course I'm excited,' said Libby grumpily, but all she could think about was her itchy head.

After supper, which was burnt sausage, drowned sprouts and soggy chips, Libby's head felt even worse.

Itch itch itch.
Scratch scratch scratch
        Scratch, scratch scratch.
Itch itch itch.

'Goodness gracious me,' said Libby's distressingly normal mum, looking up from her ironing. 'Whatever is the matter? You're itching and scratching like a flea-ridden old mongrel.'

'I can't help it, I'm allergic,' said Libby and stomped off to the bathroom.

'Oh, you poor dear,' said Libby's mum, putting down her iron and running up the stairs after her. 'What are you allergic to?'

'That new shampoo you got at shop-a-lot. Six bottles for the price of one,' said Libby grumpily, but her mother wasn't listening, because just then a strange, scorching, smell distracted her.

'What can that strange, scorching, smell be?' she said. 'It almost smells like something burning, but I've taken the custard off the stove, so it can't be that.'

'And you've already burnt the sausages, so it can't be those,' gurgled Libby, who had plunged her head in a basin of water to try to stop the itching.

It was the iron, of course, as Libby's mum discovered when she went back downstairs. There was a large neat iron-shaped mark on the back of the shirt she had been ironing for Mr Normal, ready for cousin Gertie's wedding. Since losing his job at the doughnut factory, Mr Normal had been sitting round the house with a long face. He had loved his job, which was making the holes in doughnuts, although he had always been a little bit sad that Libby only ever ate the bit he hadn't made. 'Oh dear,' sighed Mrs Normal. 'It won't show, because it's on the back. As long as he wears his jacket, it'll be fine. And perhaps the wedding will cheer him up.'

The cold water revived Libby. She felt normal again and realised that feeling normal could sometimes be quite a good thing. She bounced downstairs, her head now full of Pirate Palace.

'LOOK!' She waved Miss Wilderness's letter under her mum's nose.

Mrs Normal spent ages adjusting her glasses to peer at the letter.

Dear Parent/Carer of Libby Normal,

We are arranging a special weekend out at Pirate Palace, departing Friday May 10th at 4.30pm and arriving home on Sunday at 7.30pm. We will be travelling by coach and the whole trip will cost only £35 including unlimited rides on all attractions and two nights accommodation at Pirate Bunker. Children are expected to bring a packed tea and drinks for the coach.

To add to the excitement, as part of our literacy initiative, your son/daughter will be asked to write a short report about their day out and the best ones will be printed in the School Magazine! Please sign the slip below if you are happy for your son/daughter to attend.

'Thirty five pounds,' squeaked Libby's Mum, sitting down rather suddenly and patting her chest in an alarming manner.

Libby felt her heart flip flop right down into her flip-flops. Ever since her dad had lost his job at the doughnut factory her mum was always going on about money. Or rather the lack of money. Sometimes Libby wondered if grown ups ever thought about anything else.

'But the school will pay if we can't afford it', she said.

Her mum turned from pale to pink. 'I don't want the school knowing our business thank you very much, we'll just have to say you can't come... for family reasons... oh good,' she added, peering more closely at the letter... 'I mean, what a shame. Of course I would have found the money somehow but it's just on the very same date that your second cousin Gertie is getting married. Don't you remember? It's right in the middle of National Doughnut Week, so we thought it would take your poor father's mind off things. He always used to love National Doughnut Week.' Mrs Normal sniffed.

'Anyway, you'll enjoy a lovely wedding more than a few swings and roundabout wouldn't you?' she looked pleadingly at Libby. 'And you'll be able to wear that pretty yellow dress. Lucky I didn't burn THAT with the iron.'

Libby looked bleakly at the invitation that her mum had propped up on the mantelpiece:

Mr and Mrs Normal and LIBBY

are invited to celebrate
THE WEDDING of
GERTIE NORMAL &
ALIEN GREEN
at St Saviour's Church on Saturday
May 11th at 3pm.

Reception at THE ORBIT BAR,
OUTER SPACE CLUB.

'Isn't it funny? He's called Allen, but the printers made a mistake,' giggled Libby's mum.

'Ha. Ha,' said Libby, stomping upstairs scratching furiously. Something exciting was happening at last – PIRATE PALACE! And she couldn't go.

Instead, she had to watch her horrible second cousin Gertie marrying an alien. If only the bridegroom really *was* an alien, at least that would be fun.

Chapter Two

The next day everyone at school was jabbering away about the trip to Pirate Palace.

'It's got the scariest ghost train in the world.'

'And the biggest big wheel.'

'And the steepest rolliest roller coaster.'

'And the wildest wettest water ride. I heard they drown a couple of kids a week,' said Brainy Billy King, looking sideways at Karen, who was staring intensely at her

sandals as if they had suddenly become strawberry ice-creams.

'I'm going to spend all day on that water ride,' added Billy. 'Good place to learn my 49 times table.'

'What are you going on, Libby?' whispered Karen-next-door, not looking up from her sandals.

'I'm not coming,' said Libby.

'What?' said Karen-next-door eagerly, secretly hoping that Libby was scared to go, like she was.

'Eh?' said Yasmin, whose wiggly waggly ears had heard even from across the playground. 'Libby's not going?'

Sporty Barbara somersaulted over and did a neat back flip so she landed right in between Libby and Karen.

'Why ever not? Are you scared?"

'Of course not,' said Libby firmly. 'I have a prior engagement.' This was a phrase Libby had heard her dad using when he wanted to impress someone with how busy he was, when in fact he was sitting about the house all day with a long face.

Everyone stared at Libby.

'I mean,' said Libby, 'that I am doing something else. Something even MORE exciting.'

'What could be more exciting than Pirate Palace?

'Hah! That's for me to know and you to find out. Tell you when I've DONE IT,' said Libby mysteriously. Then, wildly, remembering the wedding invitation she added, 'but it involves ORBITS and OUTER SPACE.'

Even Billy King looked impressed by this.

'Do you know an astronaut?' he asked. His secret belief was that being a maths

wizard might help him to become an astronaut one day.

'Maybe I do, maybe I don't,' said Libby.

'Such a shame you can't come, Libby,' interrupted Miss Wilderness, who was hustling them all in from the playground. But please do write about YOUR day out at...'

'OUTER SPACE,' interrupted Libby quickly, just in case Miss Wilderness mentioned anything to do with a wedding.

Eek, what have I done? Libby thought that
night as she tossed and turned and itched
and scratched.

On Friday, Libby waved to Karen-next-
door as she went off miserably on the coach
to Pirate Palace. Libby wished and wished
she could go as she yanked on the horrible
yellow dress covered in salmon squiggles.

'Please could I wear the dress Aunt Cora

gave me?' she begged. This was a dreamy Spanish dress: red, with a flamenco dancer's skirt.

'No, dear, it's too showy, we can't have you upstaging the bride,' said Mrs Normal, who was powdering her nose. She had squeezed Mr Normal into his best suit. It was in fact his only suit, that he had bought twenty years ago for his wonderful, exciting interview at the doughnut factory.

'Breathe in, dear' said Mrs Normal as she struggled to button the jacket.

Finally Mr and Mrs Normal and Libby set off. For what was to be the most embarrassing day of Libby's life.

Chapter Three

The next day, Libby was pleased, for the first time in her life, to have to do some homework. She could forget all about the ghastly awful most embarrassing day of her life and plunge herself instead into the much more interesting world inside her head. She wrote feverishly about her day out at the wedding. But it came out a little bit, well, different.

Here's what Libby wrote:

Me and mum and dad were invited to a very grand TOP SECRET special party to launch into <u>Orbit</u> at my uncle's <u>Outer Space Club.</u>

We drove down in a stretch limo as long as a COACH.

The party started in this huge, spooky, rocket shaped building, lit up by millions of weird flickering lights, not made of electricity! And with

other flashing green and blue and yellow lights zooming about everywhere, like lasers. We were deafened by a throbbing, low, humming sound like a hippo gargling treacle.

What really happened was this:

Mr and Mrs Normal and Libby had indeed driven to the wedding in a very long vehicle. It was the local bus.

They HAD arrived at a tall rocket shaped building: St Saviour's church.

The zooming laser lights were caused the sun shining through the pretty stained glass windows. Oh yes, and the millions of little flickering lights were, as Libby said, not electric: they were candles. The hippo gurgling treacle was the wheezy old church organ, played, as it happens, by Mrs Crooke

Spindle, who has played the organ at St Saviour's weddings and funerals for the last forty years.

Libby was really enjoying her story now . Maybe it would get published in the School Magazine! She wrote on:

AND Horror of Horrors! As we entered the vast, terrifying, dismal, scary, rocket shaped building, alight with mysterious flickering flames, a terrible sight met our eyes and we froze in total terror!! We saw my cousin Gertie, all wrapped up in a long white thing like a ghostly parcel! And she was being abducted by an ALIEN!! The alien was a tall, pale grey thing with a scary, towering, vast, terrifying long thin head like a chimney! This disgusting looking creature clamped a metal ring on Gertie's poor quivering little hand. The metal ring had magic alien powers , I know it did, because the minute that the alien clamped it on her, I saw Gertie CRY!'

And then I heard someone say 'Her father's given her away!'

What? Gertie's dad had GIVEN her to the alien? No! I thought, I must save her!

What really happened:

Mr and Mrs Normal and Libby had got stuck in traffic and arrived late at the church. Naturally, they froze in horror when they realised they had missed most of the wedding ceremony and were only just in time to see Allen, the bridegroom, dressed in grey with a very smart top hat, which did make his head look very tall, putting the wedding ring on Gertie's finger.

Libby did hear someone say that her father had given her away. People always say that at weddings. It means the bride's dad takes her down the aisle and gives her to the groom.

It's true, that when Allen put the ring on her finger, Gertie did cry, which brides quite often seem to do, just like film stars and footballers do when they win, or lose, something.

Libby's story continued:

The hippo started gargling even louder to drown my cries and the horrendous chimney-headed Alien grabbed Gertie's hand in a grip of iron and dragged her FORCIBLY out of the tall spooky rocket building and THREW poor Gertie into an enormous scarlet, hovering SPACE SHIP with gigantic fiery raging fuming FLAMES shooting out of it! And the space ship shot off into the sky!

Everyone ran through the strange spooky rays of light and started waving and screaming and shouting that they were going into ORBIT and into OUTER SPACE! My dad took off his jacket to try to beat out the raging furnace and stop the spaceship from flying and his shirt got burned to a crisp! My mum started wailing and crying. And that's when I felt an alien POWER invading me!

'HELP! HELP!' I shouted. And I was overcome by a flaming, burning, agonising pain.

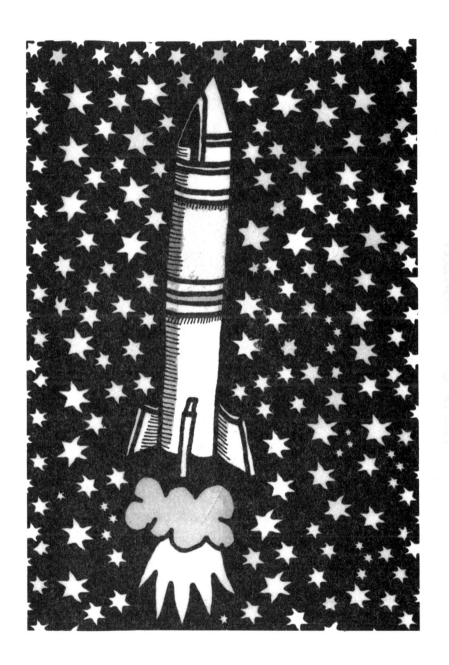

'No!' Screamed my mum! 'The ALIENS are attacking LIBBY!"
'And it was true! HUNDREDS of tiny aliens were EATING MY HEAD. They had SIX LEGS. They had horrid little holes in their sides! They had claws like razors! And they SUCKED MY BLOOD!'
Everyone at the party turned away from the spaceship to look at me in amazed HORROR! And then I fainted with the pain!

Of course, what had really happened was this:

After putting the ring on Gertie's finger Allen led her down the aisle of the church and lifted her gently in to the 'spaceship,' a lovely scarlet hot air balloon that the bride's father had hired to take the happy couple to the wedding reception at The Orbit, part of the grand Outer Space Club. There were huge flames coming from the hot air balloon and poor Mr Normal, who was already very uncomfortably hot, took off

his jacket. Everyone laughed at his burned shirt, but he didn't mind.

Mrs Normal did mind, however, because everyone else looked so very much smarter than Mr Normal. But then Libby had started wailing and scratching saying her head was on fire and one of the other little girls at the wedding party had said

'YEUK! She's got NITS.'

Everyone at the wedding had stopped

watching the lovely red hot air balloon and had turned to look at Libby instead and they all said:

'YEUK! She's got nits!'

Libby wanted the ground to swallow her up. Instead, she pretended to faint.

★ ★ ★ ★ ★

Libby sat, chewing her biro.

She did not like to remember the moment that everyone at the wedding party had said

'YEUK! She's got nits!'

It was, to put it simply, not one of the happiest moments of Libby's life.

How was she going to finish writing her story without revealing the truth? She gazed out of the window at the dreary drizzle and she thought of everyone else still having a wonderful weekend at PIRATE PALACE.

They would all come back and boast about it.

Somehow, she HAD to prove that she had had a better time, even though she had had the very worst day of her life, ever...

She took a big bite out of her doughnut, although she always felt a little bit guilty about eating doughnuts since her dad had lost his job at the doughnut factory. If only her mum wouldn't have the telly on so loud, it would help.

But just then Libby heard something on the TV that gave her inspiration. What she heard was this:

'After the news, Magician Marvin Miles uses his MENTAL POWERS to persuade people to do anything he wants!'

Hmmm, thought Libby. I'll take a break and watch that.

Chapter Four

Libby felt very cheered up after watching Marvin Miles.

He made a woman walk like a chicken and a man bark like a dog. And he did it by simply saying 'You are now in my power.'

What a useful trick, thought Libby, as she rushed to finish her story:

Then, before I could do anything another alien, this time a quivering luminous green one with a horrendous wobbly head like a green JELLYFISH grabbed me and I was taken, kicking and screaming, down a horrible spiralling ladder into a scary, slimy TORTURE CHAMBER. The green alien covered my head in a repulsive, revolting, thick, smelly cream ! I howled and cried and then the alien attacked me! With a metal bar! Covered in needles! Scraping the sharp needles across my SCALP! I screamed! But the alien continued to

scrape and push, then cackling with an eerie, screeching alien cackle, it tried to drown me in icy water! I was being brainwashed!

I knew there was only one thing for it. I was too weak to fight the aliens, but I thought I could use my MAGIC MENTAL POWERS to defeat them. I was determined to BANISH the aliens by the power of thought.

I opened my eyes wide and I thought with all my might. 'YOU ARE NOW IN MY POWER! LEAVE ME AND MY PLANET ALONE!'

And IMMEDIATELY the agonising ITCHING stopped!

The aliens had stopped eating my head!

I looked up and the luminous green alien had vanished right away! And there, instead, was my mum!

'Where's cousin Gertie?' I asked. 'Is she safe? Have they all gone?'

'Yes' said Mum, 'Gertie's fine and they've all gone.'

And it was true. The spaceship had landed and let Gertie out and she and everyone were having a party to celebrate. So me and mum went to the party. And I think the aliens had left them a cake, cos it was the tallest weirdest cake I've ever seen, about a mile high. Like a space rocket.

And when we walked in there was big cheer and everyone made speeches and cousin Gertie said how brave I was and how grateful she was that I had defeated the invaders!

Libby finished her story triumphantly.

But what had really happened was this:

When everyone at the wedding had said 'YEUK! She's got nits!' the kindly old organist, Mrs Crooke Spindle, had picked Libby up and carried her to the church toilet.

Mrs Crooke Spindle was wearing an alarmingly luminous green costume which did include a vast saucer shaped hat, with lots of wispy bits attached, the sort people so often wear at weddings because they think hats resembling jellyfish are attractive. The church toilet was on the slimy side, being at the bottom of a dank spiral staircase, but luckily it was well equipped with a first aid box including shampoo for headlice and a nit comb. This was because the choirboys at the church were constantly invaded by nits, as most small boys are.

Mrs Crooke Spindle covered Libby's

head with the shampoo, which did smell disgusting, and then combed all the horrid little nits out with the metal comb. Mrs Crooke Spindle's laugh was cackly, as old people's laughs so often are.

The freezing water was due to the church's wheezy old central heating system, even wheezier than its old organ, but Mrs Normal was there to give Libby a cuddle after Mrs Crooke Spindle had rinsed her hair clean.

And Libby, feeling much better now the itching had stopped, went with her mum and found everyone making speeches and sharing an enormous cake.

There was a huge noise when Libby entered the room, but it was not a cheer exactly, more a laugh. But cousin Gertie DID say:

'Well done! You've defeated the invaders!'

So that bit was true. And it was nice of cousin Gertie to say 'invaders' instead of 'nits.'

Libby re-read her story and felt pretty pleased with it.

'Always make the most of things,' her

mother said. And she felt she had turned a bad day into a glad day.

Chapter Five

Libby was much less happy the following day. First, everyone talked about nothing else except the very best trip they had ever had – Pirate Palace.

But worse, Miss Wilderness said she had a little announcement to make.

'I'm afraid there has been an outbreak of headlice in the school. Please take this leaflet home with you. And please all check your hair tonight.'

Everyone shoved the leaflet in their school bags, except Libby, who sneaked a look at it.

It described how headlice have six legs and breathe through little holes in the sides of their bodies and suck your blood and how you have to use lotion and a comb to get rid of them. And how their little white eggs stick to your hair and are called NITS.

Libby blushed.
She glanced round the class.
Itch itch itch.
Scratch scratch scratch.
Billy King was scratching.
Sporty Barbara was scratching.
Yasmin was scratching.

Libby was sure everyone was looking at her, even though she wasn't itching any more.

To make it even worse still, Miss Wilderness said she would read out the two best stories at the end of the day.

Libby wished she hadn't given quite such an accurate account of the aliens that ate her head. She hoped and hoped it wouldn't be HER story that was read out.

'YEUK, NITS!' said everyone at lunch.

'Why aren't you scratching, Libby?'

'You must have got them at Pirate Palace!' said Libby.

'YEUK! Pirate Palace gave us nits!' shouted everyone.

Libby used her magic mental powers all afternoon.

She stared very hard at Miss Wilderness and thought: 'You are now in My Power. And you WON'T read my story.'

YOU WON'T READ MY STORY
YOU WILL NOT READ MY STORY
DON'T READ MY STORY
DO NOT READ MY STORY

But, at 3.00, Miss Wilderness did read out the two best accounts of the weekend and one of them was Billy King's and one of them was Libby's. Which was, according to Miss Wilderness, 'VERY funny and inventive.'

Billy King's story was all about how he had taught the whole class to say their 49 times table while on the roller coaster.

'BRILLIANT of you, Billy,' winked Miss Wilderness.

Then she started to read Libby's story and Libby put her hands over her ears and tried to think of doughnuts.

But when Miss Wilderness had finished, everyone cheered.

'That was brilliant,' said Billy King.

'Cool,' said Yasmin, waggling her ears.

'Amazing,' said Sporty Barbara.

And when Mrs Normal came to pick Libby up at going home time, everyone crowded round.

'Does Libby's uncle really own an outer Space Club?'

'Did her cousin really fly into Orbit?'

'Did her Dad's shirt get burned?'

'Did those things eating her head really have six legs? And SUCK BLOOD?'

And luckily, Mrs Normal could truthfully answer 'Yes' to all these questions.

Karen-next-door came round later.

'I've just been reading the headlice leaflet,' she said. 'Isn't it funny, they sound almost exactly like those aliens that attacked you.'

'Mmm,' said Libby. 'They do, don't they? Do you want a slice of alien – I mean, wedding – cake?'